Tall Timber Tales

Paul Bunyan and his faithful Blue Ox.

TALL TIMBER TALES

More Paul Bunyan Stories

By Dell J. McCormick

Illustrated by
Lorna Livesley

19  46

The Caxton Printers, Ltd.
Caldwell, Idaho

OTHER BOOKS BY DELL J. McCORMICK:

PAUL BUNYAN SWINGS HIS AXE

First printing, June, 1939
Second printing, February, 1940
Third printing, November, 1940
Fourth printing, July, 1941
Fifth printing, April, 1943
Sixth printing, August, 1944
Seventh printing, January, 1946

Printed, lithographed, and bound in the United States of America by
The CAXTON PRINTERS, Ltd.
Caldwell, Idaho
61778

To Kirk Prindle, who once worked in
Paul Bunyan's camp.

"I cannot tell how the truth may be;
I say the tale as 'twas told to me".

Sir Walter Scott

The Growth of a Legend

HE NORTH WOODS hold many strange tales. Tales of mighty loggers. Huge, hairy men with muscles of iron. Men who broke logging chains with their bare hands and shaved with a double-bitted axe. Broad-chested lumberjacks who could fell an ox with a single blow.

Out of the woods came a tale of the mightiest logger of them all—the giant Paul Bunyan. He towered above the trees of the forest and combed his beard with a young fir tree. With his giant ox, Babe, he roamed the forests from Maine to California. His footprints were so large they filled with water and became known as lakes. When he shouted to his men whole forests were blown down with the force of his mighty voice.

His exploits are known from coast to coast. How he logged off North Dakota in a week. How he dug Puget Sound and joined the Six

Mississippis together to provide an outlet for his logs. How he invented the giant hotcake griddle and the cross-country saw that mowed down whole forests in a single day.

The men who worked with him on the Big Onion and the Little Gimlet told many tales of his mighty deeds. Johnnie Inkslinger the book-keeper, Ole the Big Swede, and Sourdough Sam. Hot Biscuit Slim, Cream Puff Fatty, and Pea Soup Shorty. Big Joe, the river boss; Broadaxe Bill, who could kick knots off a yellow pine with his bare feet; Brimstone Bill, and all the rest.

The legend of Paul Bunyan has grown from year to year. Old-timers have been questioned and logging camps searched for new material. As a result many new stories are included in the present book. Let us hope the fame of the mighty Paul will live on in the memories of the younger generation.

Stories

	Page
Preface, The Growth of a Legend	9
The Moving Forest of Bitter Root Valley	17
Elmer and the Phantom Fox	25
Paul Digs Puget Sound	33
Paul Invents Calked Shoes	39
The Lost River of Grand Coulee	49
Babe at the Circus	55
Paul Bunyan's Watch	63
The Story of Pea Soup Shorty	71
The Taming of Powder River	77
Sandy McNab and the Checkered Pants	83
Porkums the Pig	91
The Giant Mosquitobees	99
The Sawmill That Ran Backwards	107
The Story of Broadaxe Bill	113
The Six Mississippis	121
When the Rain Came Up From China	127
The Log Jam on the Big Auger	133
Paul Bunyan's False Teeth	139
Paul Goes Hunting	147
Daylight in the Swamp	153

Pictures

Page

Paul Bunyan and his faithful Blue Ox ....Frontispiece

Great fir trees were running swiftly away with little baby trees holding to their outstretched branches 16

Brimstone Bill and his crew finally locate the Phantom Fox in Paul Bunyan's beard 24

Paul decides to make Whidby Peninsula an island and digs Deception Pass 32

Big Joe rides the barked log through Big Horse Rapids and defeats Blackie Le Bois in the contest 38

Babe the Blue Ox drinks the Grand Coulee dry 48

Babe the Blue Ox becomes the main attraction of Barnum and Bailey's Circus 54

Paul's huge watch had to be wound only twice a year—on the Fourth of July and Christmas 62

Paul puts a Mississippi stern-wheeler in Bubbling Springs Lake to keep the soup stirred up properly 70

Paul gets a strangle hold on Powder River and finally chokes it into submission 76

Sandy McNab can't make up his mind whether his pants are white with black checks or black with white checks 82

Tiny Tim the Chore Boy tries his best to help, but Porkums the Pig is finally too large to enter his shed 90

The giant Mosquitobees fly away with the hotcake griddle when they are unable to withdraw their stingers 98

The smokestacks on Paul's mill were so tall they had to be hinged to let the clouds pass by 106

Broadaxe Bill tries to pick a fight with Stork Mulligan the Pacifist 112

Babe the Blue Ox pulls the log raft across the country to the Mississippi 120

13

Instead of raining down, it rained up from the ground...... 126

Babe the Blue Ox is discovered at the bottom of the huge
   log jam 132

Johnnie Inkslinger and his crew recover Paul's false teeth
   from the bottom of the sound 138

Elmer the Moosehound becomes too old to hunt and is
   carried in a special hammock to point out game 146

Tall Timber Tales

Great fir trees were running swiftly away with little baby trees
holding to their outstretched branches.

The Moving Forest of Bitter Root Valley

*P*AUL BUNYAN was probably the greatest logger in history. In fact, he invented logging and was the first lumberjack to cut down whole forests in a single week. His vast camps spread from Maine to Oregon. With his huge Blue Ox to help him Paul could log off an entire section in a day. A giant lumberjack, he towered above the trees, and it took seven men to lift his axe. Even Babe the Blue Ox was so large that he could jump whole rivers in a single stride.

Paul's camps were soon known from coast to coast. The same lumberjacks had worked for him always. Johnnie Inkslinger the bookkeeper, Sourdough Sam the cook, Ole the Big Swede, and all the rest. Many strange adventures they had together. Log jams that blocked the river, lakes of hot pea soup, and mosquito-bees with stingers three feet long. One of the strangest sights they saw was the forest of trees that walked.

It was late summer, and Paul had decided to move his camp back in the mountains where the trees were large and the streams swift and strong to carry the logs to the mills. The cook shanty and bunkhouses were tied together, and Babe the Blue Ox pulled them over the mountain passes and through the great forests as Paul and Johnnie Inkslinger went on ahead to locate a good spot for the new camp.

Late that afternoon they came to the Bitter Root Valley, and Paul saw the most beautiful tall trees he had ever seen in his life. White pine and yellow pine grew in the quiet valley. No loggers had ever set foot there, so Paul made a deal with an Indian chief who owned the land and bought the whole valley for six jackknives and a pair of suspenders.

The chief couldn't read or write. This made it rather difficult, for the government required that he sign the three hundred papers to be sent to Washington, D. C. The chief said he could sign with an X and brought out a pet turkey which he dipped in red ink and led across the papers. The turkey was trained and quickly put all the X's in the proper places.

The men were happy as they gathered around the campfire that night sharpening their axes and unpacking their long crosscut saws. Ole the Big Swede told the Seven Axemen that Paul would have a world's record cut of logs before the month was out. They all agreed that it was the finest standing timber that they had seen in all their travels.

Sourdough Sam was the first to awaken in the morning. Stretching and yawning, he went down to the creek to wash and brush his teeth. He rubbed his sleepy eyes and looked around. For some reason everything looked changed. What had happened? All around the camp was nothing but bare land. Not a tree was in sight!

"This isn't the forest where we camped last night!" cried Sam.

He could hardly believe his eyes. There must be some mistake.

"Why, the cook shanty was right over there in the center of a large grove of jack pine. I remember hanging the cleaver on a small fir tree near the cookhouse door."

He hurried back to the kitchen. The tree was gone and the cleaver was gone with it!

Quickly he called Ole the Big Swede and

Johnnie Inkslinger. They all looked around at the strange sight. Not a tree was to be found! They woke Paul and told him what had happened. Perhaps they had made a mistake the night before and camped in open country after all.

"It might possibly be a mirage," said Paul, "but we will break camp and push on up the valley to make sure."

The next day they came to another forest like the first one and again they camped for the night. In the morning the same thing happened. This was too much for Paul. He decided to find out what happened to the trees during the night and ordered Ole to stay on guard that night and call him if he noticed anything unusual.

Ole sat down near some yellow pine and waited. Nothing happened for some time. Everyone but himself was asleep. Then he began to hear a strange rustling. Dark forms began to glide past him in the forest. He thought at first it might be someone from the camp and he called to them but no one answered as they scurried on in the gloomy night.

Finally he saw it was the trees themselves

that were moving—and a stranger sight he never saw. Great fir trees were running along on their roots. Mother and father trees moving rapidly away, with little baby trees holding tightly to their outstretched branches. Once a little jack pine stumbled in the darkness and fell near him. Ole made a grab for it, but the tree gave a cry of fright and squirmed out of his arms and ran off after the others.

The next morning Paul called all the men in camp together and told them what Ole had seen during the night.

"The Indians said something about the moving forest of Bitter Root Valley, but I never believed them," said Paul.

"We are the first white men that have ever seen it. But I don't plan to let any moving forest bother my logging operations. We must find a way to catch those running trees and cut them up into logs."

Everything Paul tried was useless. Every night the trees ran away. They were willing to stand still in the daytime until the men got out their axes and saws. Then they became timid and frightened, and soon there would be a general running away. Paul tried to argue with them but it was no use. Once while he was

21

talking to a group of little yellow pines he thoughtlessly took out his jackknife and began to whittle on a stick of wood. With a cry of dismay the yellow pines all pulled up their roots and fled up the valley.

Finally Johnnie Inkslinger figured out a scheme. They cornered all the trees in one end of the valley between two high cliffs and then he had Ole and the men string cables across the valley about three feet off the ground, with the ends tightly lashed to the heavy rocks. That night Paul and all his men climbed up the cliffs in back of the trees that were huddled together. At a given signal they began to yell and throw rocks down at the trees below.

The whole forest of trees started running down the valley in one vast mad dash. Of course in the darkness they could not see the hidden cables stretched across the ground and soon they were stumbling right and left in their mad rush to get away from Paul and his men.

For hours the great pines and firs fell thundering to the ground as they tripped across the cables. Great was the noise throughout the whole valley, and people living as far away as Salt Lake City thought a thunderstorm was coming and they hid under feather beds. The force of the wind that was created by the falling trees blew owls out of trees over twenty miles away. A great dust cloud arose and hid the sun for days, and people went around pointing up in the sky and shouting, "Look at the eclipse!" but it was only Paul Bunyan and his men felling the moving forest.

Once the trees were down it was easy to saw them into logs, and in a short time Paul had logged off all the Bitter Root Valley. He left not a tree standing. To this day there is hardly a logger living who has even heard of a moving tree. Of course some of the little trees escaped and scurried back up in the mountains, but so far as is known they have never been seen or heard of since.

Brimstone Bill and his crew finally locate the Phantom Fox in
Paul Bunyan's beard.

Elmer and the Phantom Fox

THE SUMMER Paul had his camp on Tadpole Creek the cooks complained of the shortage of fresh eggs, so Paul went to work and built the largest chicken coop in the world and stocked it with eight thousand chickens. The chickens worked in three shifts, the last shift finding the nests by the aid of kerosene lamps. The tiers of roosts ran clear up to the ceiling and sometimes it took the chickens on the top row so long to get down it was time to go to bed again before they reached the bottom.

Some idea of the size of this chicken coop can be gathered from a story Shot Gunderson tells of the painter who painted the roof. It seems Paul told this man to paint the roof white and make a good job of it no matter how long it took. So he went up with his ladders, and nothing more was heard of him for several

25

years. Everybody gave him up for lost until one day a small boy climbed down the ladder and said he was the grandson of the painter and he was sent down for some more paint.

Johnnie Inkslinger counted the chickens every morning, and one day he found three or four missing. This went on for some time, and Johnnie began to suspect Sourdough Sam the cook. Sam had a special weakness for chicken pie, and they all knew it, but the little cook pleaded innocent.

"Honest, Johnnie, I haven't had a chicken pie for months, or chicken soup or chicken patties, or even a chicken sandwich."

Johnnie talked it over with Paul Bunyan, and they decided to place a guard around the chicken coop at night and find out who was stealing the chickens. Around midnight the men on guard heard a noise and rushed inside, expecting to catch Sourdough Sam red handed. Instead they caught a glimpse of a small red fox leaping nimbly through the window with a plump chicken in its mouth.

The whole camp was aroused and plans made to capture the fox. Ole suggested they spread a path of flour all around the outside of the camp the next night. In that way, if the fox returned, he would leave his footprints in the flour and they could trace him to his lair. The following night four more chickens were missing. But the strangest thing of all was that there were no footprints in the flour! The fox had not gone into the woods at all. He was still in the camp!

There was a wild scramble to look under flour bins, in wood piles and under bunkhouses, but no trace of the Phantom Fox could be found.

Suddenly Johnnie Inkslinger had a brilliant idea.

"Let's get Elmer the Moose Hound to track him to his hiding place!" he said.

Everybody thought that was a good idea, for Elmer had the keenest nose of any dog in the North Woods. He could track a fox even if the fox wore overshoes and walked backwards, as foxes sometimes do. Elmer would just sniff the ground and know exactly where the fox lived and who his father was and what he had had for breakfast the last three days.

Sourdough Sam said he remembered the day he took an apple out of the apple bin and started peeling it. Elmer, who was at the other end of camp five miles away, lifted his nose in the air and sniffed. In five minutes he was sitting happily outside the cook shanty door licking his chops, for he was very fond of apple pie. Another time Elmer was tracking a weasel, and the weasel jumped into Tadpole Creek and waded half a mile downstream to throw Elmer off the scent. Then he swam five miles upstream and came out on the opposite side of the creek —and there was Elmer sitting on his haunches waiting for him!

With a great crowd of loggers at his heels Elmer was taken over to the chicken coop. Excitement ran high, and many bets were made as to how long it would take Elmer to find the fox. It was going to be a big day for Elmer and his educated nose! But something seemed to be wrong. After sniffing around a bit he sort of gave up and quietly trotted back to Paul. They took him back to the chicken coop again and again. They showed him the window the fox jumped through. They pointed to the tracks outside. But Elmer didn't seem to be paying much attention. After a casual sniff or two he went back to Paul and refused to have anything more to do with the hunt. It was all very sad. They tried to reason with him but he just sat there looking at Paul with his great sad eyes. Everybody decided that as a fox hunter Elmer was not worth his board and and keep.

Paul called a meeting, and they all sat down to discuss the matter. Everybody had a theory, and one after another they talked and talked. It was pretty hot and Paul got tired of listening to them argue, so he lay down and soon fell asleep. On and on talked the fox hunters. The Phantom Fox was some place in camp, but no one knew where.

Brimstone Bill stood looking quietly at Elmer. Suddenly he found the answer.

"I got it! I got it! Elmer was right all along. We just didn't understand what he was trying to tell us."

Without waiting to explain he armed three or four men with rakes and clubs and told them to follow him. A ladder was placed against Paul's chest as he lay peacefully sleeping on the ground. Up climbed Brimstone Bill until he was standing knee-deep in Paul's beard.

Soon the men spread out and began beating around and poking through the heavy beard with their clubs and rakes. In less time than it takes to tell they flushed out a bevy of quail and three small chipmunks! Then suddenly a badger appeared, surly and peevish. He had built himself a nice nest in the beard and expected to stay there the rest of the summer. Up near Paul's left ear a family of small rabbits were driven from cover and went bounding off through the woods. Two raccoons scurried by as the men prowled around in the dense undergrowth of the heavy black beard.

Suddenly Brimstone Bill heard a faint rustling in the depth of the beard right under Paul's chin. He motioned to the men to gather around him. Carefully they went ahead. Sure enough, there was the Phantom Fox hiding at the very bottom where he had thought he would be forever safe from prowling eyes.

By the time Paul woke up the fox was caught and tightly tied and thrown in a cage where he would never again have a chance to steal chickens.

Elmer the Moose Hound was the hero of the camp! Wasn't he the one who had led the men straight to the spot where the Phantom Fox was hiding? It was lucky, of course, that Brimstone Bill had thought of looking through Paul's beard. Otherwise they would never have found him.

Paul admitted he had been very careless lately about combing his beard and that this

would be a lesson to him. Every morning after
that he would take a large jack pine and carefully comb his beard as Elmer the faithful
Moose Hound sat happily beside him.

Paul decides to make Whidby Peninsula an island and digs
Deception Pass.

Paul Digs Puget Sound

BABE the Blue Ox became sick one spring, and Paul knew there was only one thing to do. He decided to move west and let Babe feed on the milk of the Western whale. The whales in the Pacific Ocean were scarce that year, and Babe got steadily worse. Paul started digging Puget Sound as a grave for Babe, but the Ox suddenly got better. Paul didn't know what to do with the big hole he'd started until he met Peter Puget.

Puget suggested they go ahead and finish it and make a nice new harbor for Seattle. In fact, he had a dredge that wasn't working at the time so he took a contract to finish it in one year. Well, Peter Puget and his crew worked all one summer but they couldn't move enough dirt to fill a good-sized sandbox. He was getting very worried so he sent for Paul. The harbor wasn't big enough to float a rowboat. Paul

33

looked it over and made him a promise about the big job.

"I'll take Babe the Blue Ox," said Paul, "and dredge out a Sound that will be the talk of the whole country. When we get through there will be room for a hundred boats to tie up at docks all the way from Tacoma to Bellingham. I need room to float my logs, so I'll do it for half price and we'll call it Puget Sound because you are the man who first had the idea."

All the people roundabout had a meeting and decided to let Paul try it, but everybody thought it couldn't be done. Paul sent for Babe, and Brimstone Bill made a new set of harness for the huge Ox. Ole the Big Swede made a giant scoop shovel. It was of solid boiler plate and took the entire output of all the iron mines that year. The rivets that held it together were so large it took three men to hold them.

When it was all finished Paul hitched Babe to it with heavy logging chains and started to work. Of course he worked with a shovel himself but that was only for rounding off the corners and putting in a few islands where he thought they'd look pretty. Babe did most of the work and never seemed to object, no matter how heavy they loaded the scoop shovel. The first load of dirt was so big nobody wanted it dumped on his property, so Paul had to haul it, finally, way back in the mountains. He dumped it in two piles. By the time the Sound was completed the piles of dirt were so high they could be seen for miles, and they named them Mt. Rainier and Mt. Baker. They are still there and can be seen to this day.

Paul ran into trouble from the very beginning because everybody wanted the Sound to run in different directions. The folks down towards Tacoma wanted it extended in their direction. Then someone near Everett wanted a harbor there. It kept Paul hopping trying to satisfy them all, and that's the reason the Sound has so many turns and twists. When he was almost through he suddenly remembered he had promised to dig a harbor for some folks to the south so he scooped out Hood Canal. Funny thing too about that canal; he had just finished it and was turning around when Babe got scared of a girl standing under a red parosol and shied to the left. It made a sort of hook in the canal that is there to this day.

Finally the Sound was completed, and everyone was pleased. Paul told Peter Puget to arrange for a big celebration. They would name it "Puget Sound" on that day. Of course Peter Puget was very proud that the Sound was to be named after him and spent a lot of time getting everything ready, but the settlers had a secret meeting and decided to name it Whidby Sound and even had maps printed with the name in big letters.

When Paul heard about it he was pretty mad and he just went out with his big shovel and started filling it all up again. In no time at all most of the channel was filled in. You can get a good idea of the size of one of Paul's shovels by looking at some of the San Juan Islands. He stood there and calmly threw in shovelful after shovelful of dirt until he had almost a thousand islands dotting the Sound.

A group of settlers finally came to him and promised to change the name back to Puget Sound. He asked them who had wanted to keep Peter Puget from receiving the honor that was due him. They told him it was the people living on Whidby Peninsula. They had planned the secret meeting and decided to be selfish about it and call the new harbor after their own land. They didn't think Paul could do anything about the matter after the Sound had once been completed.

Even after the celebration the Whidby people refused to call it Puget Sound.

"Fill up the Sound!" they cried. "It won't make any difference to us. We can still haul our vegetables and milk to market along the roads."

Paul hated the way they had deceived his good friend Peter Puget so he decided to make them pay for it. At that time Whidby Peninsula was connected with the mainland by a narrow strip of land. Well, Paul just took his pickaxe and cut a narrow passage across the strip of land. The water from the Sound rushed in and filled up the passage with such force that the tides made it almost impossible to cross even in a boat. The Whidby people were cut off from the mainland forever. The channel that Paul cut is filled with raging water to this day and is known as "Deception Pass."

Big Joe rides the barked log through Big Horse Rapids and defeats Blackie Le Bois in the contest.

Paul Invents Calked Shoes

*B*IG JOE was river boss for Paul Bunyan the year they logged off the Little Gimlet just above where it empties into the Big Auger. It was quite a sight to see them ride the logs down that raging river as they balanced themselves with their long pike poles. Paul said there wasn't a braver crew anywhere and offered to bet he had the best river men in the woods from the tip of Maine to the Oregon tall timber.

Another logging outfit came to him one day and offered to back their best river man against anybody in Paul's camp. After a lot of argument they decided to settle the affair on the Fourth of July. Big Horse Rapids was the spot chosen for the contest. It was the most dangerous rapids on the river, and Paul knew it would take a good man to ride a log through that roaring water. However, the rival outfit

39

had made all the plans so Paul decided to go ahead.

In the morning there was to be log sawing and Chris Crosshaul and his pardner stepped forward as the men from Paul's camp. Two huge brawny lumberjacks from the rival camp were ready for work, with their long crosscut saw sharpened to razor edge. A yellow pine log over six feet in diameter was selected for the test. A judge stood on the log ready to give the signal to start. The first team through the log won the match.

In a few minutes Chris Crosshaul was ready. Paul noticed he was alone.

"Wait a minute, Chris. Where's your pardner? This is going to be a two-man contest."

Chris looked sort of disgusted as he spat on his hands.

"I don't want nobody at the other end of this saw. When I get to work they always gets on and rides. Don't mind that so much but they's always dragging their feet."

They finally gave the signal to start, and Chris went to it all by himself. At the same time the other two men started sawing furiously. The saws flashed in the sunlight, and great clouds of sawdust flew in all directions.

Huge brawny arms lashed back and forth as the saws bit deeper and deeper into the log. Chris was through the log before the others were hardly warmed up and said to Paul that he would have made a fast job of it but he ran into a knot.

Frank, the largest of the Seven Axemen, won the tree-chopping contest next, but the other side thought it was unfair, for the other six Axemen stood behind him, and as soon as his axe got red hot from working so fast they handed him a new axe and dipped the used one in a barrel of ice water to cool it off. In this way he worked so fast that he was able to yell, "Timber-rr!" while the other man was barely through the bark.

A log-rolling contest was next on the program. Paul chose Jean Batiste for this event. Both he and a log roller from the other camp got on a log in the river while the rival lumberjacks lined the bank cheering for their favorite. Soon the log was spinning one way and then another with each man trying to roll the other off into the icy water. Jean Batiste's feet moved so fast you could only see a blur as the log churned the water below him.

Faster and faster the log spun and faster

and faster the little legs of Jean Batiste moved with it. First one way and then the other. The two loggers seemed on the verge of going over backward into the water. Suddenly Jean stopped and quickly spun the other way. The other logger was caught off balance and plunged backward into the river. Jean Batiste was alone on the log.

"You know, Monsieur Paul," said Jean as he was being helped to shore, "I couldn't fall off that-a beeg log. You know why I stay on heem? I'm scared to fall off. You see I nevair learn how to swim!"

The final event of the afternoon, of course, was riding a log through Big Horse Rapids. This was the most dangerous contest of all, and each camp was to put up their best and bravest river man for this event. A short stocky French-Canadian named Blackie Le Bois swaggered forward. He had quite a name on the river for riding logs through white water. It would take a good man to beat him.

Paul called for Big Joe, the river boss. Joe had the heart of a lion, and Paul knew that nothing suited him better than to oppose the cocky Le Bois.

Both sides of the river were lined with loggers. Sawyers, knotters, river men, top-loaders, and bull cooks were all there to yell praises to their favorites.

A boom of logs lay above the rapids and Blackie Le Bois went upstream first to try his luck. A great cheer went up as he finally came in view around the bend. Faster and faster went the log and down it plunged into the Big Horse Rapids. Twisting and turning, it spun down through the foaming water. At times it disappeared from view in the swirling current, but always Blackie shifted his feet a bit and stayed on. Over boulders and down through the roaring whirlpools it plunged and Blackie rode it to the end. Both sides cheered as he finally came into the still water below the rapids and slowly brought his log to shore.

Paul called to Big Joe, and together they went up the river to select a log from the boom. As they passed the rival loggers there were sly smiles and whispering. Some of the bolder ones offered to bet that Big Joe wouldn't ride the log through the first turn. Others said he wouldn't last half way through the main channel. This kind of talk puzzled Paul, for he knew that Big Joe had the name of being the best river man in that part of the country.

He soon found out why they said that Big Joe would never ride the rapids that day. All the logs in the boom had been peeled as slick as so many onions. Only one log in the whole boom had bark on it and that was the log that Blackie Le Bois had ridden down a few minutes before. It was a scheme to win the contest by fraud. No man living could stand on those barked logs without slipping off into the river.

"It's a trick!" cried Paul. "Let's call the whole contest off."

Big Joe was wild with disappointment. He thought of his name on the river. He thought of the bets that had been made on him by his fellow loggers. Every greenhorn and scissor-bill would laugh at him if he failed to ride a log at all. He pleaded with Paul to let him try it anyway, bark or no bark. Paul shook his head. Just then an idea came to him. A brilliant idea! An idea that was to change the logging industry. Why not drive nails through Big Joe's shoes from the inside? The sharp points would project an inch or so through the sole. In that way he could keep his footing on any log no matter how slippery! Nobody had ever thought of doing that before.

In a few minutes he had Big Joe's shoes off

and the soles filled with nails driven from the inside out. Their sharp points caught on the peeled logs and he had as sure a footing as he could wish for. Joe gave a mighty yell!

"Throw me my pike pole! No! I don't even need a pike pole now. I'll show that tricky Frenchman a thing or two. I'll ride those rapids without a pole."

Off he went down the river, and great was the shout of surprise from the rival camp when he rounded the bend and started through the rapids. Shooting the Big Horse on a peeled log and without even a pike pole for balance! It was unheard of! It just couldn't be done.

They looked at each other in wonder. No human being could ride a log without the bark. It had never been done before. The log slipped and almost turned end for end but Big Joe clung to it in spite of everything. Down he went through the foaming whirlpools and on into the quiet water below.

Paul Bunyan's loggers cheered him wildly and carried him off on their shoulders while the rival loggers went around shaking their heads and muttering:

"It couldn't be done I tell you. It couldn't be done! And he rode the log without even a pike

45

pole. There's some trick to it, and Paul Bun-yan's put something over on us again."

From that day on Paul had nails (or calks as they were called) put in the boots of all his lumberjacks and they wear them to this day. For years the pair of calked shoes that Big Joe wore on that historic day was hanging over the door of the blacksmith shop in Paul's camp, and people came for miles around to see the famous shoes.

Babe the Blue Ox drinks the Grand Coulee dry.

The Lost River of Grand Coulee

IN THE sagebrush country of eastern Washington there's a deep canyon with towering cliffs on either side. For fifty miles it cuts its way through the desert sand. Down that deep canyon once flowed a mighty river. Its sand bars shone in the sunlight. Swirling eddies swept downstream in the swift deep current, and over a thundering falls that was higher even than the great Niagara.

Today it is called "the lost river of Grand Coulee." Tourists stand on the cliffs and toss pebbles down and hear a faint splash as they strike pools of stagnant water. Nobody seems to know what happened to the mysterious river. Even scientists disagree. A dry river bed is all that remains of one of the mightiest rivers in the West. What happened to the stream that once flowed through those canyon walls?

Paul Bunyan and his loggers knew. Brimstone Bill once told the story and the facts are sworn to by lumberjacks who first came west with Paul.

"Paul decided to move west in the middle of the summer, and it was one of the hottest summers in history. In September instead of getting cooler it began to get hotter. By December it was so hot the cooks fried eggs by just holding a skillet out the cook house window. All traveling was done at night when the thermometer got back down around a hundred and twenty degrees. I remember Paul shot a deer one day and before we could drag it into camp it was cooked to a turn and all we had to do was sprinkle on a little salt and pepper. Even the logging chains melted one day in the hot sun. The heat continued month after month and old-timers still speak of it as the Year of the Two Summers.

"Six days and six nights we traveled through sagebrush without having a drop of water to drink. Our supply had given out and we pushed on and on without seeing a well or a lake or a stream. Everyone in camp was about dead from thirst. Babe the Blue Ox was the thirstiest of all. I had charge of the Ox at the time and I knew he wouldn't be able to hold up much longer. Like all oxen he had four stomachs, but because of his greedy nature he had filled all but one of them with food when we came to the sagebrush desert. This left him very little space for water, so when the party finally arrived at the Grand Coulee River you can imagine what happened!

"Here was all the water a thirsty ox could drink! Without waiting for anyone he lowered his great head into the water and began to drink. He never even stopped for breath. He drank and he drank. He stood knee deep in the center of the river and buried his nose in the cool water. After the first few gulps the river receded ten feet. The shore line began to change. Camp cooks who were filling pails were left high and dry on the bank. The water was fast disappearing as Babe continued to drink the river dry. One of the bull cooks started to scoop up some water and got a pailful of sand. Only Sourdough Sam managed to get three barrels filled before the river completely disappeared.

"Further on down the river the loggers, after drinking their fill, had taken off their clothes and were swimming around in a deep pool below some rapids. Suddenly Big Joe noticed a woman on horseback coming along the bank. She was the schoolmistress in that part of the country and was out for her afternoon ride. Big Joe yelled at the others, and they all dived under water and stayed there with only the tops of their heads showing.

"By this time Babe had begun to drink in earnest, and the river shrank six feet with every gulp of the mighty Ox. The men in the pool began looking at each other in surprise as the water got shallower and shallower. Soon the mighty river was a mere trickling creek, and fish began to flounder along the bank. Eddies swirled no longer, and the bottom of the river began to appear. In no time at all the loggers found themselves standing in water that barely came above their ankles! Their clothes were still on the opposite bank near the schoolmistress. There was nothing to do but run for it. Pell-mell down the river bed raced the lumberjacks and finally disappeared around a bend where they hid in some willows until dark.

"Babe kept right on drinking. He was so thirsty he didn't stop until the river was completely dry. It was the queerest sight you ever saw. Great schools of fish were caught on the sand bars, and the cooks gathered them in large buckets. The roaring falls dried up to a thin trickle. Two Indians who were crossing the river below the falls in a canoe were left stranded on the river bottom and looked pretty silly as they still tried to paddle their canoe on dry land.

"After dark that night the men who had been swimming came sneaking back into camp, and Big Joe borrowed a lantern from the cook shanty to help find their lost clothes. Everybody laughed and thought it a huge joke. Even Babe looked over at Paul and slowly winked a bovine eye. The Ox was feeling good again after he had quenched his great thirst, and it mattered little to him that he had caused a whole river to disappear from the face of the earth. Yet that's exactly what happened. The river never again flowed through the Grand Coulee, and there remains today but a few stagnant pools of water where once roared one of the mightiest rivers of the West."

Babe the Blue Ox becomes the main attraction of
Barnum and Bailey's circus.

Babe at the Circus

ONE DAY a stranger appeared in camp. He said he was from Barnum and Bailey's circus and wanted to hire Babe the Blue Ox for a season. Paul thought he might just as well let the Babe go for awhile as the logging business was kind of dull at the time. Besides, his feed was costing plenty. Johnnie Inkslinger tried to figure it up but ran out of figures along about the middle of July and gave it up.

Babe had a touch of hay fever that year, and Paul thought maybe a change of scenery might do him good. Every time he sneezed he blew down almost a whole section of standing timber. One day he sneezed near the kitchen and blew a whole bin of flour out over the camp. It was raining at the time and everybody in camp got stuck in the flour paste, and work was delayed four days. Paul hated to see Babe go but anyway he told the stranger it was a deal and sent Brimstone Bill along as Babe's keeper.

The circus was playing in Denver at the time, and they set off early the next morning. Everything went along fine until they ran into some marshy country and Babe's hoofs started sinking into the soft ground. The circus man fell into one of Babe's footprints, and it was ten days before they could rescue him with a rope ladder. Brimstone Bill told him that was nothing compared with the time a whole family fell in a big footprint of Babe's out in North Dakota, and it was eighteen years before the son finally worked his way out and told about the accident.

When the Babe got to Denver, the circus people thought they had just about the best attraction in the country, for nobody had ever seen such a huge ox before. According to Brimstone Bill, who ought to know, Babe was at that time forty-two axe handles and a plug of chewing tobacco between the eyes. When he flicked a fly off his hind quarters the swish of his great tail started a wind that blew hats off people two miles away. Bill said he was a little under weight that year though and when he arrived at the circus he weighed just a little under one hundred and fourteen tons. They soon fattened him up, however, and Barnum himself came out from New York to see what the great Babe looked like.

Barnum took one look and went back to his private car, saying, "There isn't any such animal! There couldn't be. It's just something my press agent made up."

He took the first train back to New York, and from that time on he never believed a single advertisement, even if he wrote it himself.

In the meantime Babe was enjoying himself hugely and liked the circus better each day. He made friends with everybody and ate popcorn balls and peanuts. The elephants got under foot at first and he had difficulty to keep from trampling on them. He could outpull any ten elephants, and if a circus wagon became stuck in the mud it was always Babe they called on to pull it out. His great fame went before him from city to city, and each day the crowds grew larger and larger.

The circus people built a special tent for him, and it was so large it covered six city blocks and required a hundred and thirty men to put it up each time the circus moved. Twenty men kept him provided with great bales of hay. He ate so fast it took five men with pike poles to pick the baling wire out of his teeth. Every third day a wagonload of turnips was brought in for dessert. The local fire department furnished him with water in return for free tickets, but on very hot days the firemen were so busy keeping two hose carts going day and night that they didn't have time to stop and see the show.

Babe loved being the center of attraction and grew fat and sleek. He licked his glossy coat until it shone and he wanted his horns polished at least once a day. This was quite a job, for only the best steeplejacks would tackle such a dangerous task. Every day he would sit on a large platform in the center of his tent while great mobs of people would crowd in to see him. He sold photographs of himself for twenty-five cents apiece and smiled at the pretty girls and showed his fine white teeth. Every once in a while he would slowly turn his head sideways so the people in front could see his fine profile. He was very proud also of his glossy tail and brushed it regularly every morning and night.

Every day he became more touchy and complained that the food was poor and that his straw bed was bumpy. If even so much as a

58

lump the size of a popcorn ball was found in it he refused to sleep until the entire bed was changed. He refused to be in the circus parade unless he led it. If it was raining the least little bit he refused to go out and claimed he caught colds very easily. One day the little Negro who took care of his hoofs failed to show up, and Babe sat in his tent all day and sulked and would not see anybody. It was a different Babe from the good-natured Ox that had roamed the woods with Paul and his crew. Brimstone Bill began to wish they were both back in camp again.

One day the circus was playing near Minneapolis, Minnesota. He was leading the parade as usual and strutting down the main street in step to the music of the band when he met his first automobile. Here was something he had never seen before, and neither had many of the people, for the auto had just come into use. This was the first one in that part of the country. Babe did not like the fact that the auto was getting more attention than he was. He decided to look it over. He knew it wasn't a wagon because no horses were pulling it, yet it moved along by itself and made strange noises. The parade stopped as Babe carefully

59

sniffed the strange wagon. He backed away and squinted at it with one eye. He wondered whether it would be worthwhile to squash this puny thing with his great hoof. Suddenly the auto backfired.

Babe was caught off guard. It scared the great Ox half to death. With a wild roar of fear he leaped over a two-story building and started for the open country. Brimstone Bill had just time to take a firm grip on the halter rope and swing up on his back as he ran snorting and leaping through the fields north of the town. The great Babe thought only of putting as much distance as possible between himself and the new animal that made noises like a sawmill and spit fire. He was fat and overweight but he ran madly on. Whole townships were cleared in a single stride.

Brimstone Bill saw he was headed West so he gave him his head. At the rate they were going it wouldn't be long until they would be back in Paul's camp. Babe's feet were hitting the ground about once every quarter of a mile. He never stopped once to eat or rest. On and on he ran. Through forests and over mountains. Bill said afterwards it was the fastest cross-country trip ever made. The crack N. P.

passenger train had left two days before, but Babe passed it before it got to Butte, Montana. Telephone poles flashed by so fast they looked like a picket fence. Bill waved at some people standing along a country road but they were thirty miles behind before he could take his hand off the halter.

They ran into a head wind toward the end of the trip and it took Babe over two hours to cross the state of Idaho. But he made up for it in the Big Bend country, and Bill was pretty well shaken up by the time they got to Paul's camp. Everybody was glad to see them back. Bill said he enjoyed the trip except a stretch in Montana where the blackbirds were so thick they kept getting in his hair. Somebody asked him if the Rocky Mountains and the Cascades had bothered him any. Bill shook his head.

"Now that you mention it I don't think I noticed any mountains—but the trail was a little bumpy in a couple of places!"

Paul's huge watch had to be wound only twice a year—on the
Fourth of July and Christmas.

Paul Bunyan's Watch

*P*AUL heard one day that they were going to tear down the old courthouse at Tacoma, Washington, so he told Johnnie Inkslinger to go over and put in a bid for the outdoor clock on the tower.

"If it keeps good time maybe Ole the blacksmith could make it into a watch for me," said Paul.

Johnnie got there just as they were about to wreck the building and told the contractor what he wanted. The contractor was glad to see Johnnie because he couldn't figure out how to get the clock down from the tower. It was too heavy for his men to move. He thought he would dicker with this lumberjack who seemed to want it so badly.

"Well, that's a pretty nice clock, and we're proud of it," said the contractor. "Ain't another like it 'round here for fifty miles. Of course it hasn't run for fourteen years, but that makes it just like a new clock. How about fifty dollars?"

Johnnie finally found out that the contractor would pay that much just to get it off the building, so he agreed right away before he changed his mind. It took Babe the Blue Ox just two hours to lower it down with a block and tackle and before evening they had it all crated for the journey back to Paul's camp.

Ole the Big Swede was the best blacksmith in the woods and he went right to work making it into a watch for Paul. He always liked to tinker with things like that. One year up at Red Bottom Lake he made a patent alarm clock. Every morning the bull cooks would go through the bunkhouses yelling,

"Hit the deck. Roll out or roll up. Day-y-light in the swamp!" Ole never liked that method of waking the men. He said it was old-fashioned. He decided to invent an alarm clock instead that would do the work faster and better.

It was quite a machine and had several pulleys and counterweights. When it started ringing it rang for twenty minutes and then beat a gong. At six o'clock if anyone was still in bed it threw rocks at them. Several tardy sleepers were seriously injured, and Paul finally had to discard the idea.

Ole went right to work on the tower clock and inside of three months he and his helpers had the huge watch ready. When it was all finished and placed in a shiny new case it was about fourteen feet in diameter. The minute hand was six feet long and made of the finest steel Ole could buy. Paul was pleased with the job and always wore it in his pants pocket with a thirty-foot logging chain tied to a big ring at the top.

It made so much noise at first it drove three men stone deaf and scared all the deer out of the woods. Ole finally put a crew of oilers and greasers working on it until it was as quiet as any watch, and you could only hear it ticking about a quarter of a mile away. Of course with the wind in the right direction you could still hear it five or six miles away. It was a stem winder and took a donkey engine to wind it. That wasn't so bad though as they only had to wind it twice a year—Fourth of July and Christmas.

It finally stopped one winter when Paul was logging up on the Big Auger and he sent it back to Ole to have it fixed. When all the wheels and fittings were laid out on the ground they covered two and a half acres. It really was a miracle he ever got it together again, but he finally put it together and had a hundred and forty-seven parts left over, including two large circular gears that nobody had ever noticed before. Three helpers climbed into the watch and oiled and greased every moving part. When the back was clamped back in place it ran perfectly except for a slight squeak down in the lower left-hand corner. Ole crated it for shipment back to Paul up the Big Auger.

The next morning he went out to give the watch a final looking-over and nail the cover on the wooden case. Before he got the first board nailed in place, however, he heard a strange sound. A voice seemed to come from the giant watch.

"Let me out of here, you thick-headed idiot!"

Ole dropped his hammer. It was the first time any watch had ever talked back to him. He eyed it strangely. He looked under the watch. He walked around it. There was nobody but himself.

"Must have been yust the wind," said Ole as he picked up the hammer again. A watch couldn't talk! It was absurd. All a watch could do was tell time. He nailed another board in place.

"Drop that hammer, you big lummox, and let me out!"

It was the watch again! He refused to answer. What if someone came up and heard him talking to a watch? They'd think he was crazy. Ole dropped the hammer and fled. He didn't stop until he was safely back in the blacksmith shop. There he sat down to recover his breath. He was still trying to figure it out when Johnnie Inkslinger came along. He had his great notebook in his hand and he looked puzzled.

"Maybe the watch bane talkin' to Yunny Inkslinger too, by Yimminy," thought Ole.

But Johnnie Inkslinger had other things on his mind.

"I've been waiting for you, Ole. We can't find Pete Larsen, that helper of yours. He wasn't in the bunkhouse last night and he didn't show up for breakfast this morning. If he quit camp, why didn't he call in at the office for his money? Have you seen him around?"

Ole scratched his head.

"Last night yust as we quit work on the

watch he was with me and we was greasing the watch and he was inside oiling the main spring and——"

Suddenly Ole remembered.

"By Yimminy! Pete, he bane still in watch, I bet you!"

Ole started running back to the watch. With Johnnie's help he pried off the back cover of the huge watch and looked into the darkness.

"Hey, Pete! Was you down inside there?"

Out crawled the poor helper, covered from head to foot with oil and grease.

"I was yust oiling the main spring," said Pete, "when these fellars put the cover back on before I could yump out."

Paul puts a Mississippi stern-wheeler in Bubbling Springs
Lake to keep the soup stirred up properly.

The Story of Pea Soup Shorty

*P*AUL always had a lot of trouble with cooks. Cream Puff Fatty and Hot Biscuit Slim were all right, but most of the others were either baking-powder bums or sourdough dudes. Old Sourdough Sam, for instance, would make everything out of sourdough but coffee, and most of the men thought he used a little sourdough even in that.

One day two new men came into camp, and Paul put the clean one on as cook and told the other to work in the blacksmith shop. He acted a bit hasty that time, for the clean-looking fellow was actually a blacksmith but he did try his hand for a few days as cook. It wasn't any use. Everything he made turned out as hard as boiler plate. He made a batch of doughnuts one day and accidentally dropped one on the bull cook's foot. The poor fellow was laid up in the hospital for six months with three broken toes. His bread was so heavy it took six men to lift a pan out of the oven. Of course the other fellow was no good as a blacksmith, and Paul finally had them trade places.

The new cook's name was Pea Soup Shorty. He always had a big kettle of pea soup simmering on the stove. No matter how many sat down for dinner there was always enough pea soup to go around. Paul never could figure out how he managed to do it until one day as he passed the cook shanty he heard Shorty sing out,

"Throw in another bucket of water, boys. There's ten new men for dinner!"

The men sure liked his pea soup though, especially the Frenchies like Jean Batiste. The first season Shorty was in camp the peas in that part of the country dried up, and Shorty was heartbroken. He couldn't make his famous pea soup. Johnnie Inkslinger asked him to use BB shot and paint them green, for they were about the same size and the men probably wouldn't know the difference.

They did this for awhile, but it didn't work out so well. The men ate the soup all right, but they became so heavy they could hardly lift their feet. When they stumbled and fell down, they couldn't get up and had to be pulled to a standing position with a block and tackle. Paul wouldn't stand for anything like that, and Shorty had to give up the idea.

Then Shorty heard of a farmer on the other side of the next hump who had a bumper crop of peas, so he talked Paul into letting him go and see if he could make a deal for the peas. He borrowed Babe the Blue Ox and a big wagon and started out. He didn't have any trouble until he was driving back with eight tons of peas in the wagon. As they were going along Bubbling Springs Lake, the wagon got mired and turned over, spilling all the peas in the lake.

"What will I do now?" cried Pea Soup Shorty. "The men won't be able to have any of my good pea soup now that I've lost all the peas in the lake!"

He sat on the shore and sadly looked out over the lake which was fast turning green. It seemed a shame to waste all those peas. However, there was nothing he could do about it. He picked up his hat and turned to go. The hat rolled out of his grasp and tumbled in the water. Shorty reached for it and suddenly pulled his hand back in dismay. The water was hot! He had forgotten that Bubbling Springs

73

Lake was fed by hot springs. He put his fingers to his mouth. Then he licked his fingers. Why, it tasted like real pea soup! He dipped up some more from the lake and tried it again.

"Umm—this tastes pretty good at that. Now if it had a little salt and pepper——"

The whole lake was a great hot kettle of pea soup! The little cook's eyes shone. He could supply all the camps with fresh pea soup and have plenty left over. The supply would never run low.

"This will make me a name as the biggest pea soup maker in the world," said Shorty. "Paul Bunyan's camp will never want for pea soup from now on!"

He hurried back to camp and had Ole the blacksmith build a huge caldron which could be loaded on a wagon. Back and forth went Shorty, and Bubbling Springs Lake supplied all the nice hot pea soup that the men could possibly eat.

Paul later had an old Mississippi stern-wheeler put on the lake to keep the soup stirred up properly, and Pea Soup Shorty never tired of telling about his deed.

"It was my own idea," said Shorty. "I just decided all of a sudden to dump the wagon load of peas in the lake. Nobody else would ever have thought of that!"

Babe just winked his huge eye and chuckled softly to himself.

Paul gets a strangle hold on Powder River and finally chokes
it into submission.

The Taming of Powder River

ONE OF the biggest problems Paul ever had was trying to float his logs down Powder River. There was no doubt but that was the orneriest, worst-behaved river in the whole world. In the first place it was so winding and twisting it doubled back on itself every six miles. It made figure eights and great S's and crossed itself at many points. It was all very mixed up, and the men riding the log rafts would sometimes meet themselves coming back.

In other sections it ran straight for a mile or so and then turned somersaults. Naturally this threw all the logs out on the banks, and Paul was beginning to think he would never get his logs to the mills. There never was a stream like it, and old-timers say there will never be another. It ran downhill most of the time, and then all of a sudden it would turn around and run uphill. Of course some of the hills in that part of the country were too steep even for an ornery stream like Powder River and halfway up it would stop and slide back down again.

This was very annoying to Paul, and he finally planned to use Babe the Blue Ox to pull the river out straight.

"No river has ever got the best of Paul Bunyan, and Powder River will not beat me. I'll straighten out this river if it's the last thing I do!"

Everybody knew that Babe could pull anything that had two ends to it. Many's the time Paul hitched him to a whole section of timber and Babe pulled it right down to the loading skids. Babe of course was a pretty big animal. Even the iron shoes that he wore were so heavy that Ole the Big Swede sank up to his knees in solid rock when he carried one of them. Once Babe was running down a skid road and threw one of his heavy iron shoes, and it mowed down a grove of hemlock and badly injured seven Swedes who were working on a donkey engine twenty miles away.

Paul got a special iron chain made by the Krupp Iron works in Germany and tied one end of it to the river and Babe heaved and tugged and in no time at all the river was as straight as a yardstick. The strain was so great on the iron chain, however, that the links pulled out straight and they found Babe had pulled it into a solid iron bar.

Paul thought he wouldn't have any more trouble with the river after that but he was mistaken. The river refused to give up and thought of a scheme to outwit Paul. For no reason at all it would flow along as nice and proper as you please for a mile or so and then spread out over the flat country and become a mile wide and an inch deep. Just when the men on the rafts would become accustomed to this it would suddenly turn over on its back and become an inch wide and a mile deep!

Naturally this threw all the logs out on the bank again. You just couldn't do anything with a river that was a mile wide and an inch deep and then a few miles further on would be an inch wide and a mile deep! One day when Paul was lighting his pipe on the lee side of a cliff the river even had the nerve to run up the side of the cliff and pour thirty thousand gallons of water right down Paul's neck.

That was the last straw! Something must be done at once! The river must be taught a lesson it would not soon forget. Paul took off his heavy mackinaw and rolled up his sleeves. In no time at all he had a strangle hold on it and the river was whining for mercy. The minute Paul let up the least bit, however, it wiggled out of his grasp and started on another spree, throwing logs in all directions. It even buckled up and threw water over two hundred acres of farm land and flooded out thirty-two settlers.

Paul started out in chase of it, but the river had a head start and it was way out in Wyoming before Paul finally caught up with it. The river saw him coming and dived into the ground to escape, but Paul dived right in after it. They fought around for hours, first one and then the other getting the upper hand. Finally Paul got another strangle hold on it and choked it until it gave up. It was a beaten river and it knew it. From that time on it flowed quietly in its own river bed without trying any more tricks.

You can still see the evidence of that historic struggle. The earth is torn up for miles around, and a deep canyon remains where the river tried to dive into the ground to escape Paul's clutches. It is known as the Grand Canyon.

Sandy McNab can't make up his mind whether his pants are
white with black checks or black with white checks.

Sandy McNab and the Checkered Pants

*M*OST of the lumberjacks in the Big Timber country were Swedes and Norwegians though there were a few Irish. Shot Gunderson never called the Irishmen by their right names and even listed them on the payroll as Murphyson and O'Learyson and Kellyson. That's why most people got the idea Paul had only Scandinavians working for him.

There was one Scotchman however. His name was Sandy McNab, and he was very proud of his Scotch blood and wore a tam-o-shanter. He was also very proud of his fine checkered pants. They were of the finest hand-woven tweed and brought over from his native Dundee. Nothing in America could compare with these fine checkered pants. He called attention to their fine appearance and began to put on airs. The other loggers became a little tired of all this. After all, there were other pants in the world besides the checkered pants of Sandy McNab.

He continued to take himself very seriously until one night they were sitting around the stove in the bunkhouse, and Big Joe the river boss pointed to the checkered pants and said:

"I just been wondering, Sandy. Them checkered pants of yours got me worried. I'm plum tuckered out tryin' to figure something. Are they black pants with white lines on 'em or are they white pants with black lines?"

Well, that started an argument right away. Half the loggers led by Shot Gunderson held they were white pants with black lines, and the rest argued they were black pants with white lines.

"Now you take a zebra," said one of the Seven Axemen, "you wouldn't say a zebra was black, would you? Everybody that's ever seen a zebra knows for a fact that a zebra is white with black lines on it."

Tim, the chore boy, said he never saw a zebra but he had looked at a picture of one in a book he had once read called, "Life in the Zoo," and it sure looked to him as if the zebra was white with black lines. Pike Pole Murphy, or Murphyson as he was known, said he saw a zebra once at a circus, but the critter looked black to him with white stripes. He also said it had a hump on its back, so they didn't pay much attention to him, for he must have had it mixed up with a camel or a buffalo, or some other animal.

Everybody argued until it was time to go to bed, and the point was still unsettled. Long after the others had crawled in their bunks Sandy still sat looking at his checkered pants. He was a very serious soul, and a problem like this bothered him. He tried to figure it out for himself. Were they white pants with black lines or black pants with white lines? The more he pondered over it the more he worried. It began to upset him very much. He lay in bed thinking about it and for hours he couldn't go to sleep.

The next morning he awoke haggard and pale. He hardly ate anything for breakfast and kept looking at the checkered pants. Were they really white pants with black lines? He gulped his coffee and stole another quick look at the pants. No! There was no question about it. They were most certainly black pants with white lines. He could see it plainly now. Satisfied, he rose and joined the men who were setting out for the woods.

On the way to work he couldn't resist a final look at the pants. This time he knew he was right! They were white pants all right—with black lines. But a few minutes later he had changed his mind. And so it went all day long. Sandy changed his mind every half-hour and by the end of the day he was half mad with his anxiety to settle the question once and for all.

Still undecided that night, he barely ate his supper and retired to the bunkhouse to ponder the problem anew. Day after day he could think of nothing but those checkered pants. He couldn't sleep at night for thinking of them. Thirty times a day he changed his mind. He drew pictures on the bunkhouse wall and sat for hours staring at his pants and would talk to no one. Even Shot Gunderson began to feel sorry for him.

He was talking about it to Ole the Big Swede one day, and Ole thought of a fine way to settle the argument once and for all. Ole dug down beneath his mattress and uncovered a fine new checkerboard that his girl had sent him from Sweden. He took it over to Sandy. Ole felt sure he could help the worried Scotchman solve the hard problem of the checkered pants.

"See this yar checkerboard, Sandy. Ay tank ever' one here knows dat checkerboard bane white with black squares. Ya? Yust the same like yur pants. White pants with black lines. Dat bane easy for smart Swede feller to figure out."

Sandy nodded his head and smiled happily for the first time in weeks. Ole knew what he was talking about that time all right. Thank goodness the problem was settled once and for all!

Everybody felt glad that the matter was finally cleared up when Big Joe got up from his seat near the stove and went over to look at Ole's checkerboard. He ran a hairy hand through his beard and shook his head doubtfully and said:

"'Pears to me like that there checkerboard is just a plain black board with white squares— same as Sandy's pants."

With a wild yell Sandy jumped up tearing his hair and rushed madly from the bunkhouse. The problem was too much for him! His mind gave way under the strain. Night and day it had haunted him. This was the last straw. For hours he wandered in the woods. In the meantime the loggers had settled the problem for him by throwing the pants in the stove. When Sandy finally appeared, he found them gone from the clothesline where they had been drying.

He didn't seem to mind that the pants had disappeared. At least it solved the problem for him. But poor Sandy was never the same afterwards. He would not wear another pair of pants and spent the rest of the winter clad only in two heavy suits of long white woollen underwear.

He was a queer sight around the camp. The white underwear blended with the snow in the woods and he looked like a man without any legs. Everybody knew him by his red tam-o-shanter and heavy mackinaw. Further down you noticed his logging boots, but it always looked as though there was nothing in between. The swampers started calling him "No Legs" Sandy, and he was known by that name to the end of his days. At least he didn't have to worry about the problem of the checkered pants any more.

Tiny Tim the Chore Boy tries his best to help, but Porkums the
Pig is finally too large to enter his shed.

Porkums the Pig

PAUL was always fond of animals and had several pets around camp after the time he first started logging up on the Big Onion. Of course Babe the Blue Ox was always his favorite, but he was pretty fond of Elmer the famous moose-hound too. They all helped Paul in one way or another. Babe of course worked in the woods, and Elmer helped Paul on his hunting trips. Even the beavers did their share. Every winter Paul had several hundred working for him, building dams and taking care of the skid roads. They worked cheaper than lumberjacks and weren't always asking for time off.

He had six hundred and eighty beavers working for him the year he built the fence along the Great Northern Railway for Jim Hill. It seems Paul had given him a low price and promised to do the job in six months. Jim

Hill thought he'd never make it, but Paul rounded up all his tame beavers and put them to work cutting down jack pine along the right of way and chewing them up into six-foot lengths.

Then he brought in some Minnesota gophers, and the gophers started digging holes along the railroad track like they always do. As soon as a gopher would dig a nice deep hole and get it all ready for his home for the winter, Paul would reach down and pull the gopher out and drop a fence post in it. In that way he finished the job two weeks ahead of time. Of course it was kind of tough on the gophers, and some of the older ones objected and held mass meetings to complain, but nothing ever came of it. They went right to work afterwards building holes of their own, and you can still see them to this day along the tracks.

One day Porkums the pig wandered into Paul's camp up on Turtle Creek. He was a very little pig and he had become lost in the woods. Paul took him in and turned him over to Tim the Chore Boy who became very fond of him. Tim fed him on prune pits and buffalo milk, and the diet agreed with him so much he began growing by leaps and bounds. Most of the animals in Paul's camp grew to great size and so did Porkums. Even the camp chipmunks, after living on prune pits for awhile, grew so large they fought cougars and wildcats and finally became so fierce they drove all the grizzly bears out of the country.

Within a month Porkums had grown so large Tim had to climb a stepladder to scratch his back. His appetite was huge, and Tim spent most of the day carrying great loads of food from the cook shanty. Porkums grew larger and fatter and sleeker day by day until Sourdough Sam the cook could stand it no longer. He thought of the nice pork chops Porkums would make and he went to Paul and asked that Porkums be turned over to him.

"I can't look at him," said Sam, "without thinking of the juicy pork chops, the delicious bacon, the tender pork tenderloin he would make—not to mention fried ham, pork roast, pork sausage, leg of pork and pickled pig's feet!"

The cook licked his lips thinking of it and never looked at Porkums without thinking of just how many pork chops there would be for all the men and whether to have the pork roast with applesauce or cranberry jelly.

Tim had become so fond of Porkums that he didn't want to give him up and cried when Paul even said anything about it. If only Porkums wouldn't eat so much! The pig was a regular glutton and ate from morning to night. Perhaps if he wasn't so fat the cook wouldn't want him.

"Your Porkums is a glutton," said Paul. "He is eating himself out of house and home. Soon he will be so large and fat that there will be no place to keep him here in camp. He can barely squeeze through the door of his shed now. When the day comes that he can no longer squeeze through the door, I'm afraid we will have to turn him over to the cook."

Tim was heartbroken and tried his best to get Porkums to eat less, but the pig hung around the kitchen from morning to night and ate everything in sight in spite of all Tim could do. Every night Sourdough Sam watched him squeeze through the door of his little shed and his mouth watered thinking of the good meals ahead. Soon there would be a day when Porkums would fail to wiggle through the door, and Sam was eager for that day to arrive.

But the little cook waited in vain. For some strange reason the pig would waddle up to the door of his shed and wiggle through. Week after week he grew fatter and fatter but each night he could get through the door. Each time Sam would return to the cook shanty disappointed. There was no doubt but that the pig was getting fatter and fatter, but nevertheless he could always wiggle through the door at night. It was certainly a mystery! Sam shook his head and could not understand it at all. There was something queer about the whole thing! He told his troubles to Paul.

"I have given my word to Tiny Tim," said Paul, "and as long as he can squeeze through the door he is safe from your clutches."

Sam felt something was wrong, and one evening hid himself near the pig shed. He kept thinking of the fine pork chops and delicious hams he would soon have when Porkums could no longer squeeze his great bulk through the little door. He looked at the door again. It seemed impossible that the pig could ever wiggle through it that night. There was something funny about that door. Yes, sir! It looked different. What was it? Now he knew! Every night the door had been made wider!

As he sat there he saw Tim quietly approach the shed with a hammer in his hand. In a few minutes he had knocked off another board and widened the door six inches! Very carefully Tim placed the board beside the others he had already removed and placed on the ground. No wonder Porkums could get through the door every evening! It was at least eight feet wider than the original door.

Tim heard a rustling in the bushes behind him and turned around. There stood Sourdough Sam the cook!

"So that's it?" cried Sam. "Now I know why Porkums is able to squeeze through the door every night. We'll see about that, my little Chore Boy."

In spite of the weeping and crying of Tiny Tim he picked up the loose boards and nailed every one of them back in place. When Porkums waddled up to his pig shed he tried his best to squeeze through as usual. He wiggled and he twisted. He grunted and pushed with all his might. He shoved and he leaned. He lunged at the door. He turned around and tried to back in. It was no use.

The cook gleefully led Porkums away. Paul told Tim it was not his fault. If the pig hadn't been such a glutton, he would never have come to such a sad end.

The giant Mosquitobees fly away with the hotcake griddle when
they are unable to withdraw their stingers.

The Giant Mosquitobees

ONE OF the worst times Paul ever had was the time he logged off the country around Red Bottom Lake. It was nearly all swampland, and though Paul didn't know it at the time it was a famous breeding ground for mosquitoes. Not the tame, puny little kind you find back in New Jersey, but huge evil-looking insects that measured fifteen or sixteen inches from tip to tip.

The present day mosquitoes are mere pigmies compared to the ones that attacked Paul and his men during the Spring Drive at Red Bottom Lake. They appeared in swarms and began to make life miserable for everyone in camp. It was no use covering the bunks with mosquito netting. The huge insects would dive through it like tissue paper.

Paul told Ole to fit all the doors and windows with heavy chicken wire but even that didn't work. Great holes appeared in it overnight, and soon there were more mosquitoes inside the bunkhouses than outside. The small mosquitoes would crawl through the holes and help the larger ones saw an opening with their sharp beaks, like two sawyers at the ends of a crosscut saw. The beaks were sharp as razor blades in spite of the daily wire cutting, and Paul soon found out the reason. Down behind the blacksmith shop they had set up six grindstones, and while one turned the grindstone the other mosquitoes held their beaks over the wheel until all the rough edges were worn off. They had worn out three of Ole's best grindstones before Paul put a stop to it.

Paul finally decided to fight them with bumblebees and sent Brimstone Bill East for the largest and fiercest bees he could find. Bill did a good job all right and brought back six hundred of the largest bumblebees the men had ever seen. He tied their wings to their backs and took them overland on foot. It was quite a feat at that as he crossed eight hundred miles of desert and never lost a bee.

Paul turned them all loose the day they arrived in camp. Everybody expected a battle royal, but nothing happened. The bumblebees took a liking to the mosquitoes from the start and became as friendly as ants at a picnic. The bachelor mosquitoes took quite a fancy to the young lady bumblebees and soon they were intermarried right and left. The worst of it was that the offspring were twice as bad as either parent. They had stingers fore and aft and got the men both coming and going. It soon became dangerous to go out in the woods alone, and the men armed themselves with peaveys and pike poles to fight off attacks of these savage mosquitobees as the men called them.

These young mosquitobees grew to such a huge size that they began to attack the camp itself and make off with large sacks of flour and barrels of sugar. Hot Biscuit Slim put all the sugar barrels that were left in a small storehouse back of the cook shanty and tightly bolted the door, but a great swarm of the worst mosquitobees came down on it one day and carried away the sugar—storehouse and all!

Paul himself was away on a trip with Big Joe, the river boss, and the men didn't know what to do. It became a matter of life and death when the giant insects finally attacked the big dining room and started eating all the food before the men could sit down for dinner. Ole the Big Swede got the men together and led the attack against the mosquitobees, while the Seven Axemen stood at the rear door to prevent an escape. More than half the swarm was killed by the swinging peaveys and cant hooks in the hands of the angry lumberjacks.

The rest escaped through the windows and went for help. Johnnie Inkslinger bound up the wounded men and gave everybody double-bitted axes to beat off an attack should the mosquitobees return. They did not have long to wait. In less than an hour all the giant mosquitobees swarmed down on the camp. They attacked the men in battle formation and drove them from the dining room and bunkhouse. Step by step the men were driven back before the angry mosquitobees. The weary loggers finally hid beneath the giant hotcake griddle where eighteen inches of thick boiler plate would protect them from the savage insects.

The mosquitobees swarmed over the hotcake griddle, and the angry buzzing of their giant wings could be heard for miles. Finally they attacked the griddle from the top. Diving down, they drove their sharp beaks through the boiler plate with enough force to reach the men huddled beneath. When Ole saw what was happening he had a bright idea. He ordered the men to take the heavy peaveys and bend over the beaks that came through the griddle until they were flat against the under side. In that way the mosquitobees above were held fast to the griddle itself. Struggle as they could they were unable to withdraw their beaks.

More and more mosquitobees plunged their strong stingers through the griddle, and as fast as they appeared on the lower side the men bent them over and held the giant insects fast. In a short time nearly every mosquitobee in the swarm was imprisoned on the hotcake griddle, and the men below were able to relax.

The angry buzzing above began to grow to a deafening roar as the mosquitobees saw they were trapped at last and unable to escape. Suddenly the huge griddle itself began to tremble and seemed about to topple from its foundations. The men ran out from under it—and just in time too! Without warning it suddenly broke loose, and the vast swarm of mosquitobees rose in the air, carrying the heavy hotcake griddle with them!

With thankful cries the loggers watched the griddle soar away over the treetops, the mosquitobees buzzing angrily as they dragged their floating prison with them. Nothing more was heard of the giant insects until a timber cruiser two hundred miles to the south reported that he had seen the swarm slowly struggling through the air with the giant griddle weighting them down. Closer and closer to the tree-tops they flew until they finally came down in the center of Moosehead lake and quickly sank out of sight. Not a single mosquitobee escaped.

The smokestacks on Paul's mill were so tall they had to be
hinged to let the clouds go by.

The Sawmill that Ran Backwards

PAUL BUNYAN'S main interest in life was logging, and he was never happy unless he was in the woods with his men. Of course he helped Jim Hill build a railroad and he dug Puget Sound and the St. Lawrence River, but these tasks were mere side lines. He loved most to log off a section of timber that was too large or difficult for the ordinary contractor to handle.

Only once did he run a sawmill. That was down near Bend, Oregon. It was the first mistake Paul ever made, and he lived to regret it. Not many old-timers know about Paul's famous sawmill, and Paul himself never talked much about it. It was a huge affair and covered five square miles. In fact, many claim it was the biggest sawmill ever built. In spite of all the time and effort Paul wasted on it, however, it never turned out a single foot of lumber!

107

Paul went down into Oregon because he had heard of the large trees in that part of the country. He soon found that the reports were true. Those were without doubt the largest trees he had ever seen. In some places the trees were so tall that you could only see the tops on a very clear day. At that it took an ordinary man a week to see the top, or seven men working in shifts, of course, could do it in one day. The bases of the trees were so large it took a full crew of men to even chop through the bark. Paul himself started chopping down the first tree and worked all day with his huge double-bitted axe. Along about four o'clock in the afternoon he heard a faint tapping noise on the other side of the tree.

"Must be woodpeckers," thought Paul as he kept on chopping. He heard the noise again and went around to the other side of the tree to see what it was. He found two Irishmen there chopping away for dear life. They told Paul their foreman had left them there and they had been chopping on that one tree for three years and were barely through the bark. If Paul hadn't found them, they'd probably have starved to death, for their food supply was running short.

By early spring Paul had the finest lot of logs in the country, but the regular sawmill refused to cut them because they were oversize. The log carriage could only handle logs up to fourteen feet through. Of course Paul's logs were much larger than that. In fact he threw away anything under six feet as being fit only for fence posts. There was only one thing to do: buy out the mill and rebuild one large enough for the great logs he had cut.

Paul as usual decided he would do everything on a grand scale so he built a sawmill with six complete floors and a huge band saw running clear through the building from the top to the bottom. It cut logs on every floor and had teeth on both sides so he could saw the logs both coming and going.

The first trouble they had was with the smoke stacks. They were so high they had to be hinged to let the clouds go by. This took a lot of time and he finally put three men on each stack with long pike poles and they pushed the smaller clouds out of the way. It was quite a nuisance though, because it took a man so long to climb to the top that it was time to come back to supper before he was halfway up.

Paul hired an Englishman by the name of

Higgenbottom as millwright to make sure the machinery was put in according to directions. Higginbottom claimed he knew all about sawmills and could put them together blindfolded. Ole the Big Swede claimed he must have put this one together that way. Everything went wrong from the very start. Paul gave him a free hand, and he connected up saws and belts and pulleys all over the place. There were so many gadgets nobody even knew what they were for. By the time it was completed everybody was disgusted, but Paul told the Englishman to go ahead and get steam up for the opening day.

Paul was quite excited and told the chief engineer to blow the whistle. Higgenbottom had forgotten to install a whistle, so Paul grabbed an old bugle that was around camp and put it to his lips. He blew a great blast on the bugle that could be heard at Vancouver, B. C. In fact he blew it with such force he straightened every kink in the bugle until it was as straight as a flute. The machinery started moving, and the men leaped to their places.

The strangest thing began to happen! Instead of turning out lumber the mill began to take in sawdust and turn it back into logs. Vast piles of sawdust began to disappear and out of the other end of the mill, instead of finished lumber, came a steady stream of logs. Soon the mill pond was full of logs and they started to pile up on the opposite bank. The sawdust disappeared into lumber planks and the planks into logs—just the opposite to what should happen in a well regulated sawmill. They soon found out the trouble. Higgenbottom had connected everything up backwards!

Paul was very angry over the whole thing by this time and shouted to the engineer to shut down. He had all the logs he could handle already, and this crazy sawmill kept turning out more and more logs. He sent for the Englishman, but Higgenbottom had already left camp by the time they got the machinery stopped.

After trying to straighten it out without success, Paul finally gave it up as a bad job and took down the entire mill. The huge band saw was cut up into smaller pieces and used for currycombs, and the leather belting made a new set of harness for Babe the Blue Ox. Paul decided from that time on he would let the sawmill men run their own mills as they saw fit.

Broadaxe Bill tries to pick a fight with Stork Mulligan
the pacifist.

The Story of Broadaxe Bill

HE WINTER Paul logged off Minne-sota and Wisconsin he had the best lumberjacks in America. The Seven Axemen were then in their prime and thought nothing of logging an entire section before lunch. Paul had just invented a new cross-country saw that stretched for miles along the ground and cut everything in its path. It took thirty-two men working all night to sharpen it. Whole forests were cut down in a single week. Sometimes the falling trees raised such a cloud of snow the sun could be seen only on odd Thursdays.

One day a new logger came to the camp. He let them know he was there by standing in front of the main bunkhouse and roaring:

"I'm Broadaxe Bill and I can jump further and kick higher and fight better than any man in camp!"

He was a strange-looking lumberjack. He stood only five feet high and looked even shorter. He was almost as wide across the shoulders as he was tall, and his thick bullet-shaped head turned from side to side as he glared at the loggers. Nobody paid any attention to his roaring, and nothing made Broadaxe Bill angrier than being ignored. He was the toughest little camp bully this side of Quebec and he wanted everybody to know it.

Paul laughed at his boast and told him to report to Johnnie Inkslinger. It wasn't long, however, before Bill began to show that he really was a he-man logger, for in spite of his shortness he was a man of great strength. Stocky and barrel-chested, he had shoulders so wide he had to go through the bunkhouse door sideways. The calks on his logging boots were put in to form his initials, BB, and he took great delight in standing flat-footed on the bunkhouse floor and kicking his initials in the ceiling with both feet. Many of the marks are still visible today in lumber camps in upper Wisconsin.

He wore only red underwear, logging pants, and boots even in the coldest weather. Frostbitten feet never bothered him, yet winter or summer he was never known to own a pair of socks. He thought such things too sissy for a true logger. It was said he was so tough he could walk along a fallen tree and kick off the knots with his bare feet. He shaved his beard by letting it freeze and scraping it off with a hatchet.

His appetite was huge. One day he heard the dinner horn blow, and being in a hurry to get to the dining room, he dived through the nearest bunkhouse window, carrying sash and all with him as he landed in a snowbank outside.

He ate almost as much as Paul himself. Eight helpings of stew and three loaves of bread were thought a light lunch by Broadaxe Bill. Sourdough Sam complained that he was more trouble than a thousand starving Armenians. It always took two extra flunkies to wait on his end of the table.

Like all loggers he took special pride in his heavy steel axe. Every night he sharpened and honed it until the blade was as keen as a razor. He let no one else touch it and even took it to bed with him at night so the dampness wouldn't harm the blue tempered steel. He polished it every morning and removed traces of pitch with kerosene. It was his pride and joy, and he spent all his spare time keeping it in first-class condition.

Paul had a bull cook working for him by the name of Stork Mulligan. He was a tall lanky greenhorn, and one day he broke an axe handle while cutting stove wood. Sourdough Sam told him to go and borrow Broadaxe Bill's. Stork was new in camp, and the little cook thought it would be a good joke. A little later Sam went by the woodpile, and sure enough, there was the Stork chopping away with the famous axe. The cook could hardly believe his eyes.

"How come you got Bill's axe?" he asked.

"Oh, I just borrowed it," said the Stork. "I couldn't find him in the bunkhouse so I just borrowed it anyway. He won't mind, will he?"

Sourdough Sam went back hastily to the cook shanty. He had no desire to be around when Broadaxe Bill missed his pet axe. The explosion would probably tear the camp apart. He didn't have long to wait. Down the line came Broadaxe Bill bellowing his rage and threatening the scissorbill who had made away with his fine axe. He spied the bull cook cutting pitch knots. With a roar of rage he rushed for him. There was murder in his eye. The lumberjacks stepped quickly out of the way.

Stork just stood there leaning on the axe. He didn't look afraid and yet he made no move to defend himself. Broadaxe Bill stopped and glared at the bull cook.

"I'm goin' to give you the lickin' of your life!" roared Broadaxe Bill.

"I don't fight," said the bull cook.

Broadaxe Bill foamed at the mouth. He took another step forward.

"And why not?" said Broadaxe Bill.

"I'm a pacifist," said the Stork.

"And what in the blankity-blank blazes is a pacifist?" roared Bill.

"It's anyone who's too proud to fight," said Mulligan.

"We'll see about that!" said Broadaxe Bill.

He lunged forward, swinging both fists as he came. But the Stork suddenly dropped the axe and reached out with his long arms. With one hand clutching Bill's neck, he held the stocky logger at arm's length. Vainly did Bill swing his pile-driver arms. He roared and kicked and lashed out with swinging fists, but his arms struck nothing but thin air. The Stork just stood there and pushed him back as Bill came charging in. Time after time Bill rushed in, but the Stork reached out with his

117

long arms and Broadaxe Bill never got close enough to land one single solid blow.

Time after time he got up as the Stork pushed him backwards in the snow. He raged and he bellowed. His name as a camp bully was at stake but he could do nothing with the lanky bull cook who just stood there and refused to fight. It was maddening. He dived and kicked and bit. He charged with swinging fists, but it was no use. The Stork reached out with his long arms and held him at bay until his breath was gone and his arms lacked the strength to hit.

When it was all over the bull cook quietly handed him his axe, and Broadaxe Bill staggered back up the trail to the bunkhouse. The roaring laughter of the lumberjacks sounded in his ears. As camp bully he was through. He didn't stop when he got to the bunkhouse. He kept right on going until he was out of camp. It was the last of Broadaxe Bill, and none of Paul's loggers ever heard again of the barrel-chested little bully that could "jump further and kick higher and fight better than any man in camp."

Babe the Blue Ox pulls the log raft across the country to the
main Mississippi.

The Six Mississippis

THE FIRST winter Paul spent in Wisconsin he cut so many logs Johnnie Inkslinger couldn't count them all. They filled the riverbanks for mile after mile and in some places were piled so high it took a telescope to see the top logs. Johnnie used to jot the totals down on his cuff as he went from camp to camp, but one day he took his shirt off and Sourdough Sam washed it by mistake, thinking it was his own. From then on nobody knew how many logs there were.

The northern sawmills couldn't handle the output, so Paul decided to drive them down the Mississippi to New Orleans. However, at that time there were six Mississippis, not just one main river as we know it now. They all flowed south, and you couldn't tell one from another. It led to many mistakes, but nothing was really ever done about it until Paul came along.

121

When spring came he decided to send Big Joe, the river boss in charge of the first batch of logs. The men worked night and day getting the logs in the river, and Paul waved goodby to Joe and his men as they went out of sight around the first bend. Everything went along nicely for the first few days. The river was wide and swift and everybody thought they would soon be in New Orleans, but it turned out later they were on the wrong Mississippi, for it suddenly turned west and wandered all over the state of Texas. Joe and his river crew finally ended up at Alburquerque, New Mexico, and had to sell the logs to the Indians for whatever they could get.

Ole the Big Swede took another bunch of logs down the East Mississippi but he didn't have any more luck than Joe. The river turned east almost as soon as they started. It cut across Indiana and Ohio. It would flow east for a few days and then it would flow west. Then it doubled back on itself and finally emptied the logs into Lake Michigan fifty miles north of where they started.

In the meantime the sawmill owner in New Orleans kept writing and asking what had happened to the logs he had been promised. Paul was getting madder and madder. He just had to get those logs down to New Orleans somehow!

"The six Mississippis aren't going to keep me from shipping my logs south," said Paul. "I'll show them a thing or two. I'll straighten those rivers out if I have to do it with my bare hands. No river is going to tell Paul Bunyan what to do!"

The next day he chained together a great log boom and started down the third Mississippi himself. Babe the Blue Ox went along and enjoyed himself greatly, walking along the bank breaking up log jams with his great horns.

In a few days the river turned at right angles and headed West, but Paul wasn't to be fooled this time. He called to the men and they stopped the huge raft and tied it tightly to the bank. He then took great logging chains and hitched Babe to the front end. When everything was ready he shouted at Babe, and the great Ox pulled the log raft right out of the river and started across the country back to the main Mississippi.

The logs cut a deep furrow in the ground as the Ox dragged it mile after mile across the prairie. It was a mighty effort but Babe was equal to the task. When they finally launched it again they saw a strange sight. Down the furrow where they had dragged the logs came a rushing stream of water. The first river had followed the newly dug river bed and joined the two Mississippis!

When Paul saw the two Mississippis joined together he had a brilliant idea. Why not do the same to all the six rivers and make the six Mississippis one great river that would carry his logs safely down to New Orleans? It was a huge task but with Babe's help he finally did it. By dragging huge rafts of logs from one river to the other he made new river beds and turned all the rivers into the one great Mississippi as we know it today.

Instead of raining down, it rained up from the ground.

When the Rain Came Up From China

THE YEAR Paul came west he had a big camp near the mouth of the Columbia River. It was probably the biggest logging camp the West Coast ever knew. The bunkhouses stretched for miles in all directions and each had five tiers of bunks, one above the other. They were all muzzle loaders, and the lumberjacks crawled in over the ends. They were pretty comfortable too except for the woodticks.

The woods were full of ticks then, and the loggers had a hard time trying to keep them out of the bunkhouses. Those Oregon woodticks were smart too. They'd gather around the office when a new batch of loggers came into camp and even crawl down Johnnie Inkslinger's pen to see what bunk the newcomers had so they could be first to move in and enjoy it.

The dining room was a problem with so many men to feed. Ole built a giant soup kettle that covered five and a half acres and sent for the Mississippi stern-wheeler that Pea Soup Shorty had used on Bubbling Springs Lake. It was quite a sight with the fire burning merrily under it and the old steamer paddling around mixing up vegetable soup for dinner. One day a team of oxen fell in but it didn't worry Sourdough Sam any. He just changed the menu to "beef broth" that night and everybody seemed mighty pleased with the result.

The flunkies wore roller skates, but the tables were so long they used to wear out two and three pair of skates just making the rounds with hot coffee. Tiny Tim the Chore Boy drove the salt and pepper wagon. He usually drove the length of the table and stayed all night at the far end, driving back to the kitchen in the morning for a fresh load. It took so much time getting all the men into the dining room some of them almost starved to death waiting their turn. Paul finally had to build lunch counters outside where the men waiting in line could get a light lunch in the meantime.

Paul expected a wet damp winter in the Douglas fir country, but month after month went by and never a sign of rain. He had all the bunkhouse roofs lined with thick tar paper to keep out the rain. The men were given rainproof slickers to put on over their mackinaws, and Babe the Blue Ox had a big tarpaulin for his own use. It was made from the canvas of Barnum and Bailey's main tent and fitted him fine except that it was a little short around the knees.

Just when they least expected it, however, it began to rain, and it was the strangest rain that anyone ever saw! Instead of raining down it rained up! The earth fairly spouted water. It filled the men's boots. It rained up their sleeves. It went up their pant legs in spite of everything they could do. It was impossible to escape! Naturally the rain coats and the tarpaulins and the tar roofs on the bunkhouses were useless, for the rain was coming up from below.

It seeped through the bunkhouse floors and flooded the cook shanty. Men crawled into the top bunks to escape and floated from one bunk to another on homemade rafts. Hot Biscuit Slim and Sourdough Sam cooked the evening meal floating around the kitchen on flour barrels. Cream Puff Fatty sat in an empty tub and paddled back and forth to the stove cooking apple pies.

Johnnie Inkslinger looked at the yellow rain coming up from the ground and cried in great surprise:

"It's raining from China!"

Up from China came the bubbling rain until the whole forest was one vast swamp. Little fountains of water sprang up everywhere. It rained in the men's faces when they bent over to pick up a cant hook or peavey. It spurted up their coatsleeves and ran down their backs inside their heavy mackinaws. A knothole in the bunkhouse floor started a geyser of water ten feet high. Paul decided to turn the bunkhouses upside down so the tar paper roofs would keep the water out. By that time the water was well up to his ankles, which meant that it would come up to the armpit of the average man.

Just as Paul had about decided to abandon the camp the rain from China stopped as quickly as it began. The water seeped back into the moist earth, and by nightfall most of the water had disappeared except in pools here and there throughout the woods. Paul breathed a sigh of relief to find his feet on solid ground again, and the men built huge campfires to dry out their soaked clothing.

It was many years, however, before the lumberjacks in Paul's camp forgot their terrible experience with the rain that came from China. Even now when some camp orator starts to tell about a terrific rainstorm an old-timer will shake his head slowly and remark:

"Stranger, you don't even know what rain is unless you was with Paul Bunyan out in Oregon. You ain't never seen rain nor got wet unless you was working with Paul Bunyan out west the year the rain came up from China!"

Babe the Blue Ox is discovered at the bottom of the
huge log jam.

The Log Jam on the Big Auger

HE MOST daring and reckless men in Paul Bunyan's camp were the "white water" men who rode the logs down river in the spring drive. Led by Big Joe and Jean Batiste, they were as quick as cats on their feet. It was a breath-taking sight to see them leap from log to log as twenty million feet of timber shot down the foaming river. Jean Batiste could spin a log so fast that if you threw a little soap in the water, he could walk ashore on the bubbles. Big Joe could sink his calks into a small yellow pine and jump over a fair-sized rock in the river, carrying log and all with him.

Every day there were log jams that piled the river high with a creaking, groaning mass of logs—a towering mountain of logs that overflowed the riverbank and stopped the drive until the key log could be pried loose by the nimble-footed river men. Men with clanking peaveys swarmed over the pile of logs and tugged and strained until the jam loosened with a great roar and swept everything before it in a headlong rush.

Over fifty million feet of logs went into the Big Auger the day Paul Bunyan started the spring drive, and the booming and roar of the churning logs could be heard for miles. His river men worked hard poling them off the banks and clearing the backwaters. Night and day the drive continued, and men worked, slept, and ate in their water-soaked clothes.

Everything went well until the third day when Pike Pole Murphy came running up the riverbank shouting:

"A big jam is piling up down near the mouth of the Little Gimlet! We need help at once."

Paul gathered his men together and started downstream. The river was backed up for miles with a twisting, groaning mass of white pine that piled up until the top of the jam towered above the surrounding trees. The Big Auger had become a mere trickle below the jam. Giant yellow pines were upended and flung about like jackstraws. It was piling up higher and higher every minute. Paul took one look and saw it was without doubt the most gigantic log jam in the history of logging.

Big Joe and his men had worked fiercely, but the logs were wedged tightly together and the great pressure from behind kept piling them up until the face of the jam stood a sheer two hundred feet above the water.

Paul shouted for Babe the Blue Ox, but he was nowhere to be seen. Without waiting for help, Paul threw himself into the battle and began throwing the logs off the pile like toothpicks. He shoved them apart with his massive shoulders. He tossed them over his back and drove his mighty peavey into the center of the jam again and again. He pried loose great yellow pines with his bare hands.

There was something queer about this huge jam on the river. No one had seen it start, yet in a few hours it had blocked the whole river. Paul couldn't figure it out.

"Why should a log jam block the Big Auger at this point?" thought Paul. "There isn't a rock or anything for miles and miles."

Paul mounted to the top of the jam and began throwing logs off right and left. He was making progress now. Little by little, he uncovered the tightly wedged logs that formed the main body of the jam. As he threw an armful of jack pine to one side, he saw something strange in the center of the pile—two huge pointed logs. They were like no logs he had ever seen before. They weren't yellow pine or spruce or hemlock or tamarack. They were white for one thing. They curved upward to a point and were as shiny as bleached wood on tidewater. They shone in the afternoon sunlight.

Paul bent down and untangled the snarl of logs until he uncovered them more fully. Suddenly he saw them move. They swayed from side to side. Up and up they came through the mass of logs, until peering through the log jam came the face of Babe the Blue Ox! It was Babe's horns that Paul had first seen. The whole head finally appeared and the look on poor Babe's face was something to see. He was the saddest-looking ox you can imagine. Battered and wedged in the jam, he had been completely covered with the pile of logs.

Paul worked hard to free him. The heavy logs flew through the air as he untangled the huge jam. Big Joe finally gave a shout of warning. The men threw away their peaveys and scrambled for safety. A second later the jam broke, and a great mass of logs swept on down the river. Babe the Blue Ox just managed to stagger to shore in time. He was bruised and battered, and one eye was closed, but he was safe on the bank.

Paul soon found out that Babe was the cause of it all. He had become thirsty and wandered out into the river in his usual slow-footed way to get a drink. The logs in the spring drive had piled up on him before he could get out of the way. If it hadn't been for Paul, he would have been buried forever in the log jam that followed. As the weary river men rested around the campfire that night Babe quietly licked Paul's hand to show how thankful he was for the mighty effort that had set him free.

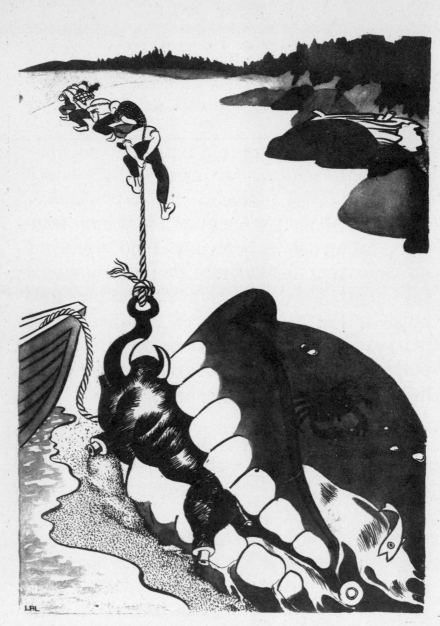

Johnnie Inkslinger and his crew recover Paul's false teeth
from the bottom of the Sound.

Paul Bunyan's False Teeth

*I*T WAS not widely known that Paul Bunyan had false teeth, and there are some who deny the story to this day. Johnnie Inkslinger, however, swore that he had paid bills for the three hundred odd pounds of ivory brought from Africa especially for the purpose. In fact, Johnnie was with him when he ordered them from a dentist in St. Paul, Minnesota.

"The dentist spent six months and wore out fifteen grindstones polishing them until they were just about the finest teeth in that part of the country," said Johnnie.

Paul was logging off the Puget Sound country at the time, and taking the teeth out there was quite a problem. Jim Hill wouldn't take them on the Great Northern because he said they were under three years old and must travel with a parent. The Wells, Fargo people

139

objected because they were too big to go in a baggage car. However, they finally loaded them on two flatcars and started them on their journey out West.

There was no trouble until the train started going over the Rocky Mountains. It was terribly cold weather with the thermometer around forty below and the snow and ice ten feet deep along the right of way. Naturally the teeth got pretty cold and started chattering. The noise kept the train crew awake all night and broke every window in the caboose. They finally covered them with blankets and quieted them down by the time the train arrived at Spokane, Washington.

Paul found the teeth fitted perfectly and was very proud of them. He used to test them for strength by biting off railroad ties, but the only time they were ever damaged was once when he made the mistake of trying to eat one of Sourdough Sam's doughnuts.

One day he was towing a boom of logs across Puget Sound and a storm blew up just as they were heading in at Point No Point. Paul hollered at Joe Batiste to throw the anchor overboard and Joe threw it overboard just like Paul said but there was no rope tied to it. Paul got pretty mad, but Joe kept on saying over and over:

"He tole me, 'Hey, Joe, throw the hank!' an' I throwed the hank. How I'm to know he want the hank tied wiz ze rope, eh?"

Paul had spent a lot of time getting those logs and he didn't want them to get away. He shouted at the top of his lungs to make himself heard above the storm. The raft was breaking up. He roared at Ole the Big Swede to lash the ends of the boom together.

Suddenly an accident happened! Ker-plop! Into the bay fell the new false teeth. Paul grabbed for them but missed! Down they sank in thirty fathoms of water.

Paul finally got the boom tied up near shore and waited for the storm to blow over. Everybody felt mighty sorry, but there was nothing they could do. Ole got a crew together, and the next day they put out in an open boat and dragged the sea bottom for miles with a huge rake, but no trace of the missing teeth was found. A deep-sea diver came up from Seattle and spent a week trying to find them but the water was too deep for his type of work.

Johnnie Inkslinger sat on the shore and thought and thought.

141

"There must be some way to get back those teeth!"

He figured with algebra and he figured with geometry. He tried to work it out with logarithms. He spent three days figuring out the tides and crosscurrents on a large chart. He sent for a book on the Japanese Current and studied it all night, only to find the next morning it was written in Japanese. He read three complete books on astronomy. He found out how to locate the Big Dipper, the Southern Cross, the Polar Star, and the Milky Way, but it still didn't tell him how to locate the missing teeth. After using up six wagonloads of paper and twenty-eight pencils, he suddenly jumped to his feet.

"I have it! I know how to rescue the teeth. It's so simple I wonder why I didn't think of it before. Ole, you get the longest cable you can find in the tool house! Shot Gunderson, you go over and get Sourdough Slim and tell him to come over here at once!"

A boat was drawn up on the shore, and Ole and his men threw in length after length of stout cable. Sourdough Sam came, and Johnnie told him to go back to the cook shanty and cook the biggest, tenderest, juiciest side of beef he had ever cooked in his whole life in the lumber camp kitchens.

"Cook it in butter! Garnish it with parsley, and flavor it well with the choicest sauce! Be sure it is well seasoned and sizzling hot! When it is done to a turn, bring it over here to the boat!"

When everything was ready, they loaded the side of beef in the large open boat and shoved off. Out in Puget Sound they rowed until they were over the spot where Paul's teeth had disappeared. Very carefully Johnnie lashed the side of beef to the end of the cable and lowered it slowly into the water. Down and down it went as the men played out the cable. Soon it sank out of sight in the deep blue water of the Sound.

Johnnie Inkslinger carefully watched the cable as it went over the side of the boat. In a few minutes he raised his hand.

"That's enough, boys. It's reached the bottom. Now row slowly ahead and we'll see what will happen."

The loggers slowly dipped their oars, and the boat moved forward. Back and forth they went, circling over the spot where the teeth were last seen.

After about an hour's rowing, one of the men

suddenly dropped his oar and leaned over the side of the boat. There was a faint noise in the water below. They stopped the boat. Soon they could all hear a faint clicking noise. It kept getting louder and louder as the boat drifted slowly. There was no doubt about it. It was the missing teeth!

In another minute they heard a loud snap and felt a tugging at the end of the cable.

"Pull away, boys!"

Johnnie Inkslinger was beside himself with excitement.

"I knew those teeth couldn't turn down a bite of good roast beef. It was always Paul's favorite meat."

They pulled with all their might, and the cable jerked and became suddenly taut. Excitement showed on every weatherbeaten face. Up and up through the blue water came length after length of wet shining cable.

Johnnie peered over the side of the boat. Suddenly with a last final pull and tug the side of beef came into view, and firmly clamped over it were Paul Bunyan's missing teeth!

Paul himself waded out to meet them, and great was his joy when he found that Johnnie and his crew had found the teeth. The whole camp was given a holiday, and everybody voted Johnnie Inkslinger the smartest lumberjack in the woods.

Elmer the Moosehound becomes too old to hunt and is carried in a special hammock to point out game.

Paul Goes Hunting

I T WAS quite a sight to see Paul with his homemade shotgun that Ole the Big Swede gave him for his birthday. It took two dishpans full of nuts and bolts to load it and used a gallon can of powder every time it was fired. On special occasions, he loaded it with a keg of nails and not only killed ducks by the hundreds but hung them pinned to trees where they could be plucked easily by the cookhouse crew.

He was a much better shot, though, with his rifle. One day he saw a deer's head pop up back of a fallen log. He shot, and the deer disappeared. Then he saw it bob up again and he fired again. As fast as he fired the deer would disappear but after a minute or so the deer would pop up again for another look. Paul was pretty much irked by this time at his shooting and went around back of the log to see about

147

it. He found thirty-two dead deer, every one with a clean shot between the eyes.

His sight was very sharp. He once shot ducks that were flying so high in the air they spoiled before reaching the ground. He spared himself that afterwards by loading his shotgun with some rock salt which kept the birds fresh until they could be picked up by the cooks. One fall, he shot some mallards so high in the air they fell across the state line and the game warden told him to quit firing at ducks so far away unless he was certain which state they were flying over.

It used to take a lot of venison to supply the camp, and Paul had quite a system for hunting deer that saved the cooks many hours of hard work. Instead of hunting them like an ordinary hunter, he would go out with Elmer the Moose-hound and round up all the deer in the forests near the camp. Then he would drive them lickety-split through the woods toward the camp and shoot them one by one as they dashed by the cook shanty. In that way Sourdough Sam had a nice fresh supply of meat right at his back door without having to send the bull cooks out in the woods to carry it in.

Elmer was getting pretty old for deer hunting though, and Paul finally had to rig up a hammock on the gun to carry Elmer. Every time the old dog smelled deer, however, he would raise up and point the direction and naturally swing the barrel in that direction too, so Paul hardly ever missed a shot even if he couldn't see the deer. When Elmer finally died, Paul got a new hunting dog that was a cross between a kangaroo and an English bull. Paul called him old High Pockets.

His front legs were only about a foot long but his hind quarters were well over six feet high. His hind legs were long and powerful like a kangaroo which made his back slope down toward his head at quite an angle. In that way, of course, he was always running downhill which made it easier for him. In fact, he never tired and could run after deer and moose for days without the slightest sign of fatigue. The deer could not get away running on the level while old High Pockets was always running downhill.

Paul used to hunt coyotes when he first came West. The state had a bounty for each one shot, but they soon had to stop that, for Paul shot so many the first day they had to mortgage the state capitol to pay him off. It was the same way with timber wolves only Paul didn't waste any gun powder shooting them. He scared them to death just hollering at 'em.

Ole the Big Swede borrowed Paul's shotgun one day and went out hunting ducks. He took just one shot, and it hurt Ole more than the ducks. The gun of course kicked back with great force and knocked Ole eighteen feet backward into some wild blackberry bushes, and it took six men to carry him back into camp. The United States Government finally mounted the gun up near Fort Casey and used it to guard the coast until the barrel wore out.

Old-timers still talk about the time Paul went hunting caribou up in Canada one winter. It was so cold everybody wore seventeen vests under their mackinaws and the thermometer dropped to four feet below zero and then froze. It was the coldest winter on record. Even the shadows froze to the ground and had to be pried loose with pickaxes. Paul put on his snowshoes one morning and went out hunting. He didn't find any caribou but he ran into some snowshoe tracks in the snow and started following them. He couldn't figure out why anybody else would be out in such weather.

After following them for miles, he saw

where they were joined by a second party on snowshoes and still later on by a third. More and more snowshoe tracks appeared in the snow until he was following a well-beaten trail. Paul followed the trail for two weeks without finding a soul and then found that one of his snowshoes had become warped because of the freezing weather and he had been walking around in a circle following his own tracks.

He finally ran into a herd of caribou, though, and got them all. They were two miles away when he first sighted them, and he tried a shot, but his gun froze. So he made a bow and arrow out of a jack pine thirty feet high and drove the arrows through their horns. In that way, he got three or four with each shot and the arrows held them together so he could swing them up on his back and carry them back to camp without much trouble. It was quite a sight to see Paul coming back over the snow with thirty-two caribou slung across his shoulders.

Daylight in the Swamp

*T*HE GREAT forests are no more. Where once Paul Bunyan and Babe the Blue Ox filled the skid roads with giant yellow pine there remains but a sea of stumps. The loggers called this "letting daylight in the swamp." Clearings appeared, and towns and villages sprang up. The spruce and hemlock no longer raise their towering branches on every mountain side. The loggers finally reached the end of the trail.

Paul Bunyan's mighty crew is scattered to the four winds. Ole the Big Swede and Brimstone Bill went to work for Weyerhaeuser. Pea Soup Shorty and Sourdough Sam joined the Red River Lumber Co. and are probably still cooking hotcakes in northern California. Big Joe, the river boss, rides the Columbia River log rafts for the Long-Bell outfit.

Paul himself logs no more in the great

North Woods. With Babe the Blue Ox and his faithful dog, he hunts and fishes high up in the Olympics. On a summer evening they say you can hear him shout, and the trees still bend and sway with the force of his mighty voice. Rocks and boulders crash down from the side of Mt. Olympus when he takes his morning walk. His logging days are over, and he has well earned his rest.

Many a hunter has tried to find the spot where Paul now lives with his great blue Ox. But the high Olympics guard well the secret of his final hunting ground. To reach it one must pass through the Valley of the Echos where every word is magnified a hundred times. The slightest noise echoes and re-echoes until the valley is filled with a sound like thunder. The snapping of a twig underfoot becomes as loud as a shot fired from a cannon. Most hunters refuse to camp in the valley, for the noise of the echoes has been known to drive men mad.

Beyond the Valley of the Echos lies the Canyon of the Rolling Stones where huge rocks and boulders come crashing down the slopes and no man's life is safe. Not a single hunter has ever passed through the canyon though many have tried. Beyond the canyon lies the camping ground of Paul Bunyan where he hunts and fishes with Babe the Blue Ox. His logging days are over, and he is at peace with the world.

The spirit of Paul Bunyan lives on in America, and no task becomes too great or difficult when we think of the hardships Paul endured and the mighty exploits he performed. Gone forever are the days when Paul Bunyan logged the great North Woods. There's "daylight in the swamp" from Maine to California.